WAR OF THE WORLDS

Adapted by
Charlotte Fullerton
from the screenplays by
Dwayne McDuffie

SCHOLASTIC INC.

NEW YORK TORONTO LONDON AUCKLAND
SYDNEY MEXICO CITY NEW DELHI HONG KONG

ISBN-10: 0-545-17715-4
ISBN-13: 978- 0-545-17715-3

12 11 10 9 8 7 6 5 4 3 2 1   9 10 11 12 13 14/0

Cover art by Min Sung Ku and Hi-Fi Design
Designed by Rick DeMonico
Printed in the U.S.A.
First printing, September 2009

Space. The vast and beautiful cosmos fills the view in every direction with its infinite star systems, colorful nebulae, and strange worlds. The majesty of outer space is truly a wonder to behold.

Suddenly, there is a tremendous jolt that shatters the silence. In a blinding flash of light, a seemingly endless fleet of battleships arrives in an area of the universe known as the Galvan System. These powerful spaceships are HighBreed Destroyers, and they immediately target this system's most prominent planet, the glowing green world called Galvan Prime. The armada of warships enters the world's atmosphere like a swarm of locusts.

On the surface below, in a futuristic alien city, a group of tiny, gray, bug-eyed creatures wearing white and black robes has gathered, staring up into the night sky. They are fearful and agitated. These little aliens are Galvan, the life-forms who call Galvan Prime their home.

Lightning strikes. An ominous shadow passes over the crowd, obscuring them. Overhead, the Galvan see the source of the shadow—the swarm of HighBreed Destroyers!

A prominent tower displaying a familiar green and black hourglass symbol overlooks the threatened city. One particular Galvan stands here apart from the others, watching the terrible scene unfold before him. He looks exactly the same as his fellow Galvan assembled below, except his robe is green and black, echoing the symbol on his tower. Clearly this Galvan is special somehow.

The Galvan doesn't even blink when a burst of blue energy suddenly explodes in the room behind him. Nor does he react when a thin, trim human male wearing a white lab coat walks out of the glow before it fades.

"Azmuth, come with me," says the intruder calmly.

Azmuth answers without turning around. "There's no point, Time Walker. The HighBreed armada caught us totally by surprise. Galvan's planetary defenses are down. We don't have a chance." The little alien finally turns to look back at his visitor. "And without the Galvan, no other race in the galaxy has a chance either."

The human smiles as he walks to Azmuth's side. "But, and I hesitate to say this to the smartest being in the universe, that's where you're wrong."

"Explain," counters Azmuth.

"We do have a chance," the man reminds him. "The chance you made for us."

"That is not what the Omnitrix is for," states Azmuth firmly.

But the human will not be deterred. "The boy has proven more than once that it can be used for purposes beyond what you intended."

Azmuth considers this. "Perhaps."

"Come with me to Earth," the man entreats him.

The Galvan shakes his head. "I'm not leaving my home. Not now." He turns to look out the window again.

His human friend joins him. "And I'm not going back without you."

They watch grimly as first one, then all of the ships begin to fire powerful energy weapons at the city. The glowing red beams sweep slowly but inexorably through the streets, tearing through buildings like butter, obliterating everything in their path.

As the man and the alien watch, one destructive beam begins heading toward them. They say nothing as the beam comes closer and closer. They are almost lost in the glow. Azmuth's city is in flames, but he's determined to see it out to the bitter end. And the end is coming fast!

The man turns and, looking down at his alien friend, without a hint of panic in his voice says, "I sincerely hope you'll reconsider in the next three seconds or so."

As the invading HighBreed's red energy beam approaches the window, a flash of blue light engulfs the two figures. Seconds later, the blast hits Azmuth's tower and blows it into a million pieces!

Meanwhile, on a planet known as Earth, in a town called Bellwood, a high school soccer field is bustling with activity. It's nighttime, but the field is lit by huge banks of bright lights providing almost as good visibility as daylight.

Bellwood's goalie, number 10, readies himself to block a shot from one of his own teammates. He catches the ball in his gloved hands with a grunt. This is fifteen-year-old Ben Tennyson. He is average height for his age, athletic, with dark brown hair and striking green eyes. "I'm all warmed up. It's game time!" he announces, throwing the ball back into play.

"I'm afraid the time for games has passed, my friend," says a solemn voice. The man in a white lab coat has suddenly appeared at Ben's side.

"Professor Paradox?" Ben says. The man in the lab coat and Ben already know each other, for this is the eccentric time-traveling scientist Ben and his friends shared an incredible adventure with in the past.

"And one other," says Paradox as Azmuth steps out from behind him.

Ben gasps in amazement. But before he can ask any questions, Paradox says urgently, "Come with me."

A few minutes later, this unlikely trio enters the parking lot of Mr. Smoothy, Ben's favorite hangout. Ben's fifteen-year-old cousin Gwen and their sixteen-year-old friend Kevin are waiting for them. Kevin's beloved green sports car, a classic 1970's GTO, is parked nearby.

Gwen and Ben have shared many adventures together over the years. When they were ten years old, they spent one fateful summer vacation with their Grandpa Max. It was then that Ben and Gwen first learned about the existence of aliens from other planets, as well as about Grandpa Max's years of policing the universe as a member of a secret society called the Plumbers.

That was also the summer Ben was first chosen to be the wielder of the most advanced piece of alien technology ever created, a watch-like device called the Omnitrix. It was invented by the very same little Galvan standing with him now under the eerily cheerful Mr. Smoothy sign. Using the power of the Omnitrix to transform into ten of the many different alien creatures stored in its DNA database, Ben became a hero involved in galactic adventures beyond his wildest dreams.

A lot has happened since then, not the least of which is that Ben's cousin Gwen has learned that her seemingly magical abilities are actually energy-manipulating powers she inherited from their grandma, who was an alien. And the biggest change of all: Their onetime enemy, Kevin Levin, is now their friend and ally, who uses his amazing ability to absorb any kind of solid matter to help Ben, Gwen, and the Plumbers defend the innocent against hostile aliens.

As for Grandpa Max, he hasn't been seen since the kids left him back in the prison dimension, the Null Void, a place with which former bad guy Kevin is all too familiar.

"What's so important that I have to miss the auto show?" Kevin complains. He may not be evil anymore, but Kevin still has his own priorities.

"The imminent destruction of your primitive world and all who live there," Azmuth retorts.

"But if you'd rather go look at a new convertible, by all means," Gwen chides him.

Ben interrupts the bickering. "Professor?"

"The HighBreed attack has already begun," Paradox says.

"We know," Ben interjects. "We've been fighting them for weeks."

"The situation has escalated," Azmuth explains. "They have conquered my home world, the only planet with the technology to fight them head-on."

Ben asks, dreading the answer, "And their next target?"

Paradox nods grimly. "Earth."

Azmuth fills in the details. "The HighBreed attack plan, simple-minded though it is, has worked on a dozen worlds. They send a small number of HighBreed to the target planet. . . ."

"Then they infiltrate the locals by turning them into DNAlien slaves," Paradox finishes.

Kevin gets it. "And use the slaves to build a Jump Gate."

"Correct," Azmuth nods. "A Hyperspace Jump Gate is an interstellar shortcut, allowing the HighBreed to send warships across the galaxy in a matter of seconds."

Ben hesitates, worried. "The three of us could barely take down one of their ships."

"The ship you defeated wasn't a warship," Paradox corrects him. "It was a small cruiser."

"That's encouraging," responds Ben sarcastically.

"No force on this planet could stand against even a single HighBreed warship," Azmuth states emphatically. "They will send hundreds."

"Yeah, okay, we get it," Kevin sighs. "We're hosed."

"Unless we stop them before they complete the Hyperspace Jump Gate," says Paradox.

"It should be simple enough to find," muses Azmuth, "even if they cloak it."

Paradox continues Azmuth's train of thought. "It would have to be someplace with an enormous supply of quartz crystal, to stabilize the matter transmission frequency."

Gwen snaps her fingers in recognition. "You mean like the abandoned quartz mine in Los Soledad?"

Ben makes the connection too. "Where we saw DNAliens building a giant arch."

Kevin is all business. "So we know where we gotta go, and we know what we gotta do."

Gwen is ready to go for it too. "Direct approach."

Ben reins them in. "Sure. Direct, but not stupid." Ben pulls off his soccer jersey. "We've met a bunch of Plumbers' kids with superpowers, and a lot of them owe us favors." He puts on his green jacket. "I say we call them in."

Azmuth offers some advice. "May I suggest you send your teammates out for that job?"

"Why?" asks Ben.

"I would have words with the wielder of my Omnitrix," says Azmuth cryptically. "In private."

Kevin leans against his car. "Right. Like I'm going to miss this. See you when you get back, Gwen." Gwen grabs Kevin's arm and yanks him. "Hey!"

"Kevin Ethan Levin!" Gwen scolds him. "You come with us right now!"

"'Ethan'?" Ben grins. Your name is Kevin *E. Levin*? You just lost all remaining pretense of cool!"

Reluctantly, Kevin joins Gwen and Paradox. All three begin to glow in Paradox's trademark blue light.

Kevin looks accusingly at Gwen as they start vanishing. "You promised you'd never tell!"

That same night, stalks rustle in a cornfield on the outskirts of Bellwood. Someone is running through them. It is a twelve-year-old African-American boy, Alan Albright, making his way quickly through the tall creepy corn. He thinks he hears something and stops, listening carefully.

More rustling. It's not him making the noise this time. Is it the wind? Alan doesn't think so. He reaches out with both hands and pulls apart the tangle of corn stalks in front of him. It's a DNAlien! The hideous creature roars at him aggressively, the tentacles on its face quivering with menace.

But Alan is not impressed. "Yeah. Whatever."

In a burst of fire, Alan transforms himself into Heatblast II, a fiery lava alien form not unlike one of Ben's past alien forms. Like Gwen, Alan inherited his amazing interstellar attributes from a family member who was an alien.

Heatblast II conjures up a fireball in his hand and poises to hurl it at the DNAlien. "So, you want to go a couple of rounds, or just give up?"

Uncharacteristically, the DNAlien squeals in fear, turns, and runs away, speeding through the stalks of corn.

"My reputation precedes me," chuckles Alan.

As the DNAlien disappears into the cornfield, Heatblast uses a large, flat-topped stone to surf through the air. Looking down, he sees the DNAlien's path through the cornfield. Heatblast projects a swath of flame into a circle around the DNAlien. He's got it trapped! The DNAlien protests loudly in its own language, which Alan can't understand.

"Yeah, yeah," Heatblast mutters. "Tell it to the sheriff."

"Nice work, kid," says Kevin's voice from behind him. A little farther back, enclosed in Paradox's glow, are Paradox and Gwen. "But if you really want to make a dent in the alien problem, you should come with us."

Back in the parking lot of Mr. Smoothy, Ben and Azmuth are deep in conversation. The little gray Galvan stands on the trunk of Kevin's car with a Mr. Smoothy to-go cup beside him. It's almost as big as he is.

"Humans are not the brightest species in the galaxy," Azmuth says calmly, as if stating a simple fact. "So I ask you again: Do you fully understand the risks you are taking?"

"Sure," Ben says matter-of-factly. "The HighBreed want to take over the Earth."

"The HighBreed want to *destroy* the Earth," Azmuth corrects him. "If you lose this war, it's the end of humanity!"

"So I won't lose," Ben says, shrugging.

Azmuth wags an angry finger up at his young pupil. "Your foolish disregard of the enormity of the odds against you is precisely why I cannot allow you to take the Omnitrix into battle!" The mastermind of the Omnitrix looks quickly from side to side, needing to be absolutely certain this next part is not overheard. "I have told you that the secret of the Omnitrix is it allows you to walk a mile in the shoes of other life-forms. This is not the complete truth."

CHAPTER THREE

In the basement of his parents' house, a chubby young genius named Cooper is busily working on his latest scientific experiment. Cooper is an old friend of Ben and Gwen's. In the past, he's helped them battle aliens using his telekinetic abilities, not to mention his super smarts.

The cellar is packed with dozens of computers and a whole assortment of high-tech gadgetry of Cooper's own design. He is wearing a strange mechanical-looking gauntlet on his left hand. Cooper knocks on a big steel plate standing in the middle of the lab. It's completely solid.

"Here goes nothing!" he mutters.

Cooper switches on the glove, and his hand goes semi-transparent! He gingerly puts the hand right through the piece of steel.

"Works like a charm!" Cooper smiles with satisfaction.

"Cooper?"

Cooper spins around to see Gwen has appeared behind him, along with Paradox, Kevin, and Heatblast.

"Gwen!" Cooper gushes. He has a huge crush on her. "How'd you get in here? Oh, I don't care, it's great to see you!"

Cooper runs over to hug her, but his arms pass right through her. "Oh." He steps back and presses a button on his gauntlet. "Intangibility glove," he explains as his arms go solid again. "Still experimental, but I can use it to create an exception field to three-dimensional physics, defying—"

Gwen interrupts gently, trying not to hurt his feelings. "Maybe you can tell me about it later. I need a favor."

"Anything for you, Gwen."

Kevin rolls his eyes. "You hear that, Gwen? 'Anything.'"

"Give him a break, Kevin," Gwen says. "We're asking him to risk his life."

Cooper presses on, undaunted. "Kevin's juvenile teasing doesn't bother me in the least. My adoration for you is far too pure and strong to—" Suddenly, Gwen's words sink in. "Risk my life?"

"We're going back to Los Soledad to fight the HighBreed," Gwen explains. "You don't have to if you don't want to."

"If you're going," resolves Cooper, complicated circuitry patterns suddenly glowing in his eyes, "then so am I."

As he speaks, mechanical devices from around the room levitate toward him, reshaping themselves. A moment later, Cooper is dressed for battle in a souped-up, battle-armored robot suit!

Back in the Mr. Smoothy parking lot, Ben is staring at Azmuth in disbelief. "You lied to me?"

Azmuth picks up his Mr. Smoothy cup and sips from the straw. "I withheld portions of the truth from you until such time as you were ready."

"And I'm ready now."

Azmuth frowns. "No. But circumstance has forced my hand. The Omnitrix is the last hope of alien species destroyed by the HighBreed."

Ben shakes his head, not understanding. "How's it supposed to—"

Galvan interrupts him. "I have stored within it DNA samples of every intelligent life form in the Milky Way galaxy."

"Ten thousand of them," says Ben, nodding. "I know."

"As I'm continually forced to point out, you know very little," sighs Azmuth. "There are over one million samples encoded in the Omnitrix."

This is news to Ben. "A million?"

"And with the Omnitrix," Azmuth continues, "you have the power to return to life any species that the HighBreed exterminates." Azmuth looks Ben in the eye. "Including the human race."

"I will not let the HighBreed—" Ben begins.

Azmuth cuts him off. "If you are destroyed with the Omnitrix, there is no hope. Not for humanity, nor for any other race the HighBreed extinguishes afterward."

Ben tries to take it all in. He's overwhelmed.

Azmuth continues gravely, "The Omnitrix is Noah's Ark, and you are Noah. I cannot allow you to participate in the final battle."

Crickets chirp in the crisp night air outside the Mt. Rushmore National Memorial near Keystone, South Dakota. But this historic monument hides a secret. Inside, it's a Plumber base, fully tricked out with cutting-edge technology for monitoring all alien activity on Earth and engaging in battle with hostiles.

In one corner of the base, Professor Paradox, Kevin, Gwen, and Heatblast are watching Cooper set up a high-tech warp projector.

Kevin is growing impatient. "How long is that gonna take?"

Cooper, kneeling by the device, replies, "Almost ready." He looks over at Gwen. "You're sure you want me to do this?"

Gwen nods. "Ben said all the help we could get."

"Okay," Cooper agrees, "switching on." He presses the control in his hand, activating the device.

A tube of crackling red energy, a Null field, shoots straight up in the air, revealing trapped within it none other than Mike Morningstar, one of Ben, Gwen, and Kevin's greatest enemies. He is wearing the iron head mask he adopted in his evil incarnation, Darkstar. After his last encounter with Ben and his friends, Darkstar was sent to the Null Void prison dimension.

"Free!" Darkstar bellows as he flings himself at the tube of red Null Void field energy encasing him. He bounces back in pain. "Ah!"

"Save yourself the trouble, Darkstar," Kevin warns his former competitor for Gwen's affections. "You don't get out of there unless we say so."

"Kevin Levin," Darkstar smirks behind his mask, "and the lovely Gwen Tennyson. To what do I owe this unexpected pleasure?"

"We're here to free you from the Null Void," Gwen says.

"Why?" Darkstar can't imagine. "You put me in here in the first place."

"Much as I'd like to take the credit," Kevin replies, "Ben gets the glory on that one."

Gwen gets to the point. "There's a threat to Earth. Ben needs your help. We all do."

"And if I promise to help you?" Darkstar asks coldly.

"We let you out," Gwen promises. "Simple as that."

Darkstar keeps his cool. "Then we have an agreement, lovely Gwen."

"Let him out," Gwen tells Cooper.

Cooper frowns. "I don't like the way he talks to you."

But Gwen is adamant. "We need him, Cooper."

With a grunt of disgust, Cooper throws a switch and the Null Void field disappears, leaving Darkstar standing before them, unbound.

Darkstar slowly approaches Kevin, and they stare each other down for a long, tense moment. Finally, Darkstar turns away. "Why would you trust me?" he asks cynically.

Kevin snaps back, "I don't. But now that you're on Earth, if you don't help us, *you* won't survive either."

CHAPTER FOUR

Ben and Azmuth are inside Kevin's parked car, Ben in the driver's seat, Azmuth riding shotgun. They've been talking for a long time.

"Sorry, Azmuth, but I don't buy your argument," Ben says, shrugging. "The Earth needs to be saved, and I'm going to do it."

Azmuth crosses his itty-bitty arms and firmly stands his ground. "I won't allow it."

Ben asks, honestly wondering, "How could you stop me?"

The Galvan looks up at Ben with resolve. "I'll take the Omnitrix from you!"

Ben raises the wrist that has the Omnitrix and hovers his other hand over the activation panel. He's ready to use it on a moment's notice. "You'll try."

Azmuth gives Ben a long look and realizes that Ben isn't going to be talked out of this. "Very well. If you insist on this foolishness, perhaps it's best if you have the full power of the Omnitrix."

The creator of the Omnitrix now turns his attention to the watch. "Access Master Control."

The Omnitrix pulses with green bubbles of other-worldly energy, then speaks in a voice that sounds exactly like Ben's. "Master Control Unlocked. Command and Control fully available to Ben Tennyson."

"Everything's unlocked?" Ben blurts excitedly. "How many aliens can I turn into?"

The Omnitrix answers in Ben's own voice, "One million nine hundred and three genetic samples available."

"The Omnitrix's menus are arranged in sets of ten for simplicity's sake," Azmuth explains. "But with voice command, you can—"

"Got it," Ben interrupts, grinning.

Suddenly there is a violent *thump-thump-thump* on the roof of the car. It's Kevin. "Get out of my seat, Tennyson."

Gwen sticks her head in the window. "We brought some help."

Standing behind Kevin and Gwen are Professor Paradox, Heatblast, Cooper in his robot suit, Darkstar, and Ben's non-superpowered, tennis-champ girlfriend, Julie Yamamoto.

Julie waves casually. "Hi, Ben."

Ben leaps out of the car and rushes over to her. "Julie? What are you doing here?"

"You need help," Julie reminds him.

"And you can help . . . how?" wonders Ben.

Julie sticks her fingers in her mouth, whistles, then calls out, "Here, Ship!"

The sentient alien blob of Galvanic Mechmorph material known as Ship eagerly scampers over to Julie. Ship was left behind here on Earth by a marooned creature similar to one of Ben's past alien forms, Upgrade. Ben rescued Ship and this alien during his and Julie's first date. "Ship Ship Ship Ship Ship!" chirps Julie's pet.

Julie pats Ship on its head, encouraging, "Do your trick."

Immediately, Ship begins transforming into an immense warship—the same form that another enemy, the Forever Knights, once forced him to assume. Now, instead of chirping happily, Ship's voice is deep and menacing. "Ship!" the warship booms.

Ben looks at the enormous, heavily armored vehicle that is Ship, then at Julie, and concedes, "Oh. Okay."

Kevin's classic sports car rolls to a stop in the abandoned desert town of Los Soledad. He, Ben, and Gwen pile out.

Some of our heroes have been here before. Not too long ago, Ben, Gwen, and Kevin rescued Cooper from the clutches of some DNAliens who were holding their friend prisoner. The DNAliens were forcing Cooper to use his hyper-intelligent, telekinetic mind to build a cloaking device to hide their operations in Los Soledad from prying eyes. Now Ben knows they were building a Hyperspace Jump Gate to bring the HighBreed armada to Earth!

Mechanically enhanced Cooper strides up to join Ben. Ship lands, and Julie runs down the gangplank, followed by Paradox. Heatblast flies in, then Darkstar emerges from Kevin's car. The Alien Force is ready for action!

"Why are we stopping here?" Darkstar wonders. The place appears to be completely deserted.

Cooper uses the enhanced vision of his suit to reveal the dome of energy that's covering the town. "It's a cloaking field."

Kevin touches his car to get himself ready for battle, absorbing its green steel until it covers his entire body. "Once we go past here, it's on!"

Ben turns to face his team. "Okay. Nothing fancy here. We go in. We destroy the Hyperspace Jump Gate. We capture any HighBreed we can find. That's it."

He raises his hand to slap the Omnitrix, then pauses and turns back to his team. "One more thing. Whatever we were before, today we're a team. We look out for each other. We win or lose together."

Ben slaps the Omnitrix, and a blinding green flash engulfs him. Inside the Omnitrix, the DNA of Ben's human form is altered, merged with that of the alien he has chosen to become. Surrounded by bubbling green energy, Ben's back, shoulders, and hands swell, transforming his features from those of a teenage boy into those of a strange and powerful creature. His eyes narrow, and his human face widens until it seems it might split. When the transformation is complete, Ben announces his name in the creature's voice, "Cannonbolt!"

Gwen gazes in surprise at this squat, white alien form with large orange pads at its joints and back. "Haven't seen him for a while."

"What can I say?" Cannonbolt jokes. "I'm feeling nostalgic."

Cannonbolt lumbers up to the border of the cloaking field and steps through it.

On the other side of the invisibility cloak, snow is falling. Gwen steps through to join Cannonbolt, then Paradox and Darkstar follow, along with Heatblast and Mecha Cooper, and warship Ship with Julie. Finally, Kevin slowly drives his car in.

"They've been busy," Kevin remarks, looking around.

The entire city has been transformed into a DNAlien staging center. The arch is complete, with running lights on the ground below. Weather towers are everywhere, just like the ones Ben, Gwen, and Kevin came across way back when they first met Alan as Heatblast. And though it was a clear night outside the cloak, thanks to the weather towers the DNAliens have constructed, it's snowing in here.

Darkstar catches a snowflake in his palm. "Snow?"

"The aliens like it cold," Gwen explains, shivering. "I should have brought a jacket."

"I've got a feeling it's going to get pretty hot in here," Cannonbolt says.

Just then, a small group of DNAliens notice the intruders. They drop what they're doing and let out a high-pitched screech, calling to the others. More and more DNAliens pop up all over town. There are hundreds of them here, maybe thousands. And they're all stampeding toward Ben and his friends!

Darkstar immediately fires black energy rays from his hands, taking down every DNAlien he hits. Cannonbolt rolls up into a ball and barrels into several more. Gwen projects snaking tendrils of manna life-force energy from her hands. Mecha Cooper stamps through another battalion. Yet still they keep coming!

Some of the creatures hold blaster weapons and fire at the intruders. Metallic Kevin drives his car right into the approaching hordes of DNAliens, zigging and zagging to dodge their blasts. A few DNAliens open their disgusting tentacled mouths and spit out globs of sticky resin at Kevin's car. Armored for battle, Kevin bails out and goes hand-to-hand with the DNAliens, punching his way through their ranks.

With powerful energy glowing around each hand, Gwen blasts her way past a bunch of other DNAliens. To avoid their retaliation, she quickly creates two floating magenta energy plates in the air ahead of her and hops on for a short ride, one foot on each. She continues to attack the enemies from above, then lands without missing a stride.

Under heavylaser fire from the armed DNAliens below, Metallic Kevin climbs the water tower. Then he leaps all the way down, landing hard, causing a large section of the pavement to break free. He heaves the boulder he's created at the DNAliens.

Overhead, Heatblast sky-surfs, firing flame blasts from both hands down into the crowds of DNAliens.

Ignoring the laser blasts, Cannonbolt runs forward, curling into a ball, then rolls into another big group of DNAliens, scattering them like bowling pins.

Several more DNAliens hack up resin balls and spit them at Kevin, who watches in horror. With a swipe of her hand, Gwen quickly creates a force shield to protect him.

Kevin seizes the opportunity to leap over the shield as far as he can, smashing more pieces of pavement into boulder-sized debris with his landing.

Dozens of DNAliens fire their laser blasters right at Paradox at point-blank range. The Professor calmly checks his pocket watch, stopping time for everyone but himself. He walks briskly between the many laser blasts hanging frozen in midair, then past his motionless assailants.

Tiny, gray Azmuth dodges a barrage of laser fire and resin. One glob manages to hit him and sticks the little guy to the ground. And an entire legion of DNAliens is marching right toward him!

Just in the nick of time, Paradox reaches in and pulls Azmuth out of the goo. Together, they escape the DNAliens' resin balls by entering one of Paradox's space-time warps, disappearing and reappearing in a blur.

Cooper uses the enhanced vision of his robot suit to lock onto dozens of the DNAliens' laser rifles. He presses a button, causing every DNAlien in his sights to blow up in a deafening explosion!

Overhead, Julie stands smugly, arms folded, on top of warship Ship. Any DNAliens who come near her get the ground in front of them blasted to smithereens by loyal Ship, whose deep voice repeats his name as he flies through heavy enemy laserfire.

Darkstar is blasting several DNAliens with his Dark energy, which looks like the opposite of Gwen's energy fields. His victims writhe in pain on the ground. One DNAlien manages to land a single punch, knocking Darkstar's iron helmet cleanly off his head into the snow. He crumples to the ground.

With weapons drawn, the DNAliens approach their fallen victim. He rolls over to reveal the hideously distorted facial features his mask had hidden.

Darkstar explodes in fury. A column of black energy erupts into the air, hurling DNAliens in all directions! When their bodies land, Darkstar swoops in to drain the life force out of them.

Drawing the unconscious DNAliens' energy to his hands in crackling electrical streams, Darkstar levitates off the ground triumphantly. The massive energy boost restores his original handsome looks to his ruined face. "Yes!" This is the moment Darkstar has been dreaming about ever since he was locked away in the Null Void.

Cannonbolt rolls over and unfolds from his ball shape.

"No! Stop hurting them!"

"This is a battle," Darkstar scoffs. "We do what we must to survive."

"These are human beings, Michael," Cannonbolt says sternly. "They're under alien control. We take them down, not out. Understand?"

Reluctantly, Morningstar stops draining the DNAliens. A moment later, his face is withered again. Embarrassed by his shattered looks, he puts his iron mask back on. "You're a fool, Ben. What would you do, cure them?"

Cannonbolt thinks about this for a second. "Actually, that's not a bad idea!" Cannonbolt touches the Omnitrix symbol on his chest and says, "Omnitrix, revert DNAliens to human."

A green beam lances out of the Omnitrix and strikes a DNAlien, who reverts back to his human form. He's alive but unconscious.

The Omnitrix speaks in Ben's voice. "Genetic damage repaired."

Cannonbolt is weakened by the effort, but now that he's seen that it works, he's got to keep trying. "Again," he pants, winded. "As many . . . as we can."

The beam fires several times, striking and curing more DNAliens. Cannonbolt leans forward, palms on his knees, trying to stay upright.

The Omnitrix issues an alert, "Warning: Energy reserves depleted. Cycling to recharge mode."

Cannonbolt does not want to give up. "Again," he commands weakly.

But the Omnitrix symbol on his chest changes from green to red, signaling it is out of energy. Cannonbolt swoons and passes out face-first in the snow. As he hits the ground, he turns back into Ben.

Before Gwen or Kevin can reach him, DNAliens stalk Ben, surrounding him. They pull out futuristic ray guns and open fire!

CHAPTER SIX

The laser blasts from the DNAliens' ray guns unexpectedly ricochet off a magenta energy dome that suddenly appears over Ben's unconscious form. It is Gwen's handiwork. Metallic Kevin sneaks up behind the DNAliens and knocks their heads together. They collapse to the ground, out cold.

Darkstar fires at other DNAliens creeping along the rooftops as Gwen crouches next to her unconscious cousin. "Ben, are you okay?" she prods him gingerly. Ben moans.

Kevin pats him on the cheek, hard. "Wake up! Much as you need your beauty sleep, now's not a good time."

Ben snaps awake. He shakes his head to clear it. "What happened?"

A blur whooshes in and coalesces beside the three teens. It is time-warping Professor Paradox with Azmuth.

Azmuth folds his arm. "You misused the power of the Omnitrix!"

Ben doesn't see what he possibly did wrong. "I was helping people!"

The creator of the Omnitrix is not impressed. "You were wasting power in a pointless exercise."

Paradox smiles kindly, showing Ben his pocket watch.

"Good intentions, Ben. But in matters like this, timing is everything."

"What do you mean?" asks Ben.

The Professor says simply, "It will come to you."

The battle is raging all around them. Cooper and Darkstar provide cover while the conversation continues.

Ben can't believe this. "Are you saying I can't use the Omnitrix to cure the DNAliens?" He looks down at the device, which still blinks red instead of its normal green, its energy temporarily used up.

Mecha Cooper chimes in helpfully, "Now that I've seen how you do it, maybe you don't have to."

Mysterious circuitry patterns begin to glow in the boy genius's eyes. Cooper raises his giant mecha arms, and his exoskeleton telekinetically breaks apart, its pieces hovering individually in the air around him. It's as if he's in a trance. Radiating a powerful blue energy, Cooper gestures wildly with his hands, causing all the loose parts to shuffle around and reassemble themselves into an array of very cool new ray guns. They hang in the air, floating in a ring around their creator.

Cooper, now himself again, plucks one of the new weapons out of the air.

"What are those?" asks Ben.

"I call them Bugzappers," Cooper says. He pivots and fires at a DNAlien Kevin is holding, striking the creature with a green beam. The energy instantly transforms the DNAlien into a human woman! She falls into Kevin's arms, unconscious.

Kevin is suitably impressed by Cooper's new invention. "Oh, I like that."

"One shot will revert a DNAlien to human," Cooper explains.

"And it won't hurt them?" confirms Gwen, plucking one of the Bugzappers out of the air.

"They'll wake up with a little headache," says Cooper, firing another shot.

Everyone grabs a Bugzapper except Ben, who dials the Omnitrix to Jet Ray and slaps the watch face. In a flash of green energy, Ben is gone, and the Aerophibian he has chosen to become is zooming straight up into the sky, a Bugzapper in each hand. "Jet Ray!" the creature announces. Jet Ray soars high over Los Soledad, firing his two Bugzappers at the dozens of attacking DNAliens below.

Jet Ray transforms in midair and free-falls down into a pile of DNAliens as another alien form. "Swampfire!" he calls out, continuing the barrage without a pause. Then, aiming a powerful blast of fire straight down, Swampfire blasts off into the air like a rocket.

Elsewhere in the battle, Gwen shields herself with a magenta energy field with one hand and fires a Bugzapper at DNAliens with the other.

Professor Paradox strides calmly through the melee, firing a Bugzapper. Riding on his shoulder, Azmuth tries to wield one of his own, but it far outsizes him, and he topples to the ground.

Darkstar blasts his dark energy beams from one hand and fires a Bugzapper with the other.

Heatblast, gliding overhead on an energized chunk of smoldering debris, hurls waves of fire down with one hand and fires a Bugzapper with the other. He causes volcanic cracks to form in the ground, erupting with hot lava that sends the DNAliens running!

Julie, riding on top of warship Ship, aims her Bugzapper at the scattering DNAliens and picks them off one by one as Ship sails expertly through a hailstorm of enemy laser blasts.

Swampfire flings handfuls of thorns at a firing line of DNAliens. But instead of acting as shrapnel, the thorns implant in the ground at the DNAliens' feet, growing instantly into undulating green vines! Swampfire waves his hands to control them from a distance, making the gigantic vines wend around the DNAliens like tentacles. The vines raise the enemies high into the air, where Cooper can get clear shots at them.

Meanwhile, in the slush on the ground, little Azmuth struggles to hoist his Bugzapper. He manages to get off a single shot, but the recoil knocks him backward and bounces him away like a pogo stick.

Kevin charges into battle, rapid-firing a Bugzapper in each hand. All around him, DNAliens are illuminated with green energy as they are hit, then transformed back into human beings.

The Alien Force is doing it! Working together, our heroes blast their way through the sea of DNAliens, changing their enemies back into people.

But up on a platform close to the Jump Gate, two DNAliens are setting up what looks like an anti-aircraft ray gun. They lock onto Swampfire and fire!

Swampfire sees the blast heading for him. Quickly, he activates the Omnitrix from the symbol on his chest and transforms into another of Ben's old aliens, Upchuck!

The short, round creature leaps into the air, opens his mouth, and swallows the oncoming laser blast. His stomach swells, his cheeks bulge, and he vomits the energy back at his attackers! It hits the anti-aircraft ray gun and destroys both it and the platform in a tremendous explosion. The DNAliens dive for cover.

Inside the HighBreed control room, the HighBreed Earth Commander is watching the fight on his monitors. He's enraged, barking orders to two other HighBreed.

"It's impossible. That vermin must not be allowed to reach us!"

One of his DNAlien lackeys stammers nervously, "Our forces are routed, master. I–I do not think we can stop them."

"Very well. We must accelerate our plans," decides the HighBreed Commander. "Activate the Jump Gate now!

A strange, purple-and-orange pod-like structure rises up from the floor between these two HighBreed. They place their hands into the pod, creating patterns that light up the control room with an orange glow.

As lightning crackles in the sky overhead, Upchuck, Gwen, Kevin, and their team approach the base of the Jump Gate. A series of orange lights along the edge of the Arch begins winking on.

Gwen is the first to notice. "Guys! The Jump Gate's powering up!"

"What do we do now?" asks Alan.

"We break it!" shouts Kevin. He hurls himself at the arch. It rings like a gong, but is unaffected. Kevin bounces off and lands in the snow. "Not a scratch! What's it made of?"

Paradox knows. "Nutronium-carbon alloy."

Kevin shakes his head. "Dude, that was totally . . . what's that word?"

"Rhetorical," offers Gwen, helping Kevin to his feet.

"Yeah, that," Kevin agrees.

Upchuck has an idea. "Everybody hit it together. On three. One, two, three!"

All the heroes combine their powers on a single spot on the arch. The fusillade lasts several seconds then the dust clears.

"Nothing," reports Darkstar grimly.

He's right. The arch is a little scorched where they attacked it, but is otherwise unharmed.

Cooper is concerned. "Maybe we're too weak."

Upchuck says defiantly, "Maybe not!" In a flash of green light, stocky little Upchuck is gone. In his place, standing tall, is another of Ben's old alien forms. "Waybig!"

The towering alien grabs one base of the arch and begins trying to uproot the whole thing! The ground where it was connected cracks and crumbles under the strain.

"It's working, Ben!" Gwen shouts. "Keep trying!"

Waybig strains with effort. As he struggles, the landing lights running parallel to the arch begin to blink in a regular pattern. The arch itself begins to glow.

Paradox sees it and panics. "Ben! Back away!" he shouts. "It's about to—"

The Jump Gate discharges a huge electrical arc. Waybig is trapped within the field as it charges with electricity. He's being electrocuted! The crackling electrical currents tear open a warp hole in space under the Arch.

Waybig staggers away from the Jump Gate and falls backward. His friends hurry out of the way to avoid being crushed.

As the Alien Force watches in horror, a long stream of HighBreed Destroyers pours out of the Jump Gate. In moments, the sky is filled with HighBreed battleships.

The invasion of Earth has begun!

CHAPTER SEVEN

Waybig lies perfectly still on the ground. There is a flash of green light, and then he's gone.

Lying in the trench created by the force of Waybig's fall is Ben Tennyson—battered, bruised, and unconscious. Groggily, he stirs and slowly opens his eyes, then reacts in alarm. The sky above him is filled with HighBreed battleships!

The Alien Force team rushes to his side. Gwen slides down the dirt wall of the trench and skids to a stop in front of him.

"We're too late!" she laments, offering Ben a hand.

"It's never too late," Ben counters. "New plan."

Everyone looks expectantly at Ben, who after a long, uncomfortable silence continues, "Working on it."

"That's reassuring," Kevin sighs.

Ben snaps his fingers. "Got it! We break into the HighBreed Control Room and force the HighBreed Captain to make his ships retreat."

"Seriously," Darkstar asks incredulously, "that's your big plan?"

"How many times have I beaten you?" Ben reminds his former enemy.

"Twice," Darkstar admits. "But just this moment, I can't imagine how."

"The main control tower will be the most heavily guarded building in the city," Azmuth warns.

"Precisely my point," says Darkstar. "How do you propose to get inside?"

Kevin grins. "Leave it to me."

A moment later, the door of Kevin's car slams closed with a satisfying thunk. Kevin settles into the driver's seat. Gwen and Ben are already inside, riding shotgun and buckled into the backseat, respectively.

Gwen crosses her arms in irritation. "We're going to drive to the control tower?"

Kevin just smiles and nods. "Uh-huh." He hits a control button, and the car's dashboard begins to transform, revealing alien tech readouts. Black and green computer circuitry patterns similar to the designs on Ship begin spreading across the ceiling of the car. Then the car itself transforms, displaying a diverse combination of alien technology that includes missile launchers, plasma beam projectors, et cetera. Kevin's GTO is a rolling arsenal of alien tech!

"When did you get all this stuff?" asks Ben, amazed.

"When *didn't* I?" Kevin shrugs. "Every time we found some alien tech, I tossed it in the trunk, and whenever I have free time—"

"You work on the car," Gwen says, nodding.

Kevin turns and smiles rakishly at Gwen. "Yep." He steps on the gas pedal and the car squeals away, heading right into the remaining horde of DNAliens.

Kevin begins firing the car's weapons in every direction. He uses missiles, pulsating energy beams, automatic fire energy bursts—every kind of alien tech Kevin has ever been able to get his hands on. The DNAliens try to fire back with their ray guns, but beams from Kevin's car blow up the ground at their feet, sending them flying.

So the DNAliens get organized. They pull an eighteen-wheeler truck into the car's path.

Ben gulps nervously as the car zooms toward the truck's flank, still traveling at breakneck speed. "You're not going to stop, are you?"

"Nope," states Kevin, his eyes fixed firmly ahead. He thumbs a control on the dashboard, firing a rocket that demolishes the side of the truck in a ball of fire. Only now their car is headed right for the fireball!

Gwen uses her manna-controlling powers to generate a magenta energy sphere around their car just as Kevin floors it, launching the GTO off the ground! The car emerges from the other side of the fireball and slams back down to the ground.

"And *this* is why we always wear our seatbelts," Ben comments.

"Nobody likes a backseat driver," Kevin grumbles.

The HighBreed armada blanketing the sky above begins to rain down laser fire on the GTO. Kevin swerves to avoid being hit, nearly losing control of the vehicle. Missiles explode all around as the car careens wildly through the streets of Los Soledad, crashing right through buildings and anything else that stands in the way.

At last, they skid to a stop at the bottom of the stairs leading to the control tower. Ben, Gwen, and Kevin climb out.

"Run to the control room. Then we fight," instructs Ben.

"I was afraid you were going to say that," Kevin says sadly. He reaches into the car and presses a red button on the dashboard marked AUTO ATTACK. His car races off all by itself.

A troop of DNAliens line up in formation and fire laser blasts at Kevin's unmanned vehicle. But the car doesn't waver. It just keeps driving straight toward enemy lines. The car deploys its missiles at the attacking DNAliens, engulfing them in a tremendous explosion.

"That'll hold 'em for a while," Kevin says. He, Ben, and Gwen make a beeline for the stairs to the control tower.

Kevin's car is still putting up a good fight on its own, but it's taking a lot of heavy damage from DNAlien ray gun blasts. Kevin stops running to watch what's happening to his beloved GTO.

Gwen notices him dawdling and grabs his shoulder. "Kevin, come on!"

"I'm going to miss that car," Kevin says sadly.

A moment later, he and Gwen have caught up with Ben. They follow him up the long, thin row of steps leading to the Control Tower.

"The HighBreed have starships, but they haven't invented the elevator?" Gwen grouses.

When they finally reach the top, they stop in front of an imposing door of alien design. Kevin touches the wall and absorbs it, covering himself in stone, ready for battle.

Ben dials the Ómnitrix and selects the hologram of Swampfire. "It's hero time!" he says confidently, slamming his palm down.

Instantly, vines sprout from where Ben's hands had been and twist their way up his arms, mutating his human limbs, torso, and head into strange alien foliage. "Swampfire!"

Swampfire's hand ignites, and he wields it like a flamethrower at the sealed door before them.

Inside the Control Room, the HighBreed Earth Commander, his assistant, and several DNAliens turn to see the door glowing red-hot and melting away, revealing Gwen, stone-covered Kevin, and Swampfire on the other side.

"Tennyson!" snarls the HighBreed Earth Commander. "That *is* you, isn't it? All of you lesser species look alike to me."

"Yeah, yeah, you're all superior and pureblooded and we're all maggots," replies Swampfire dismissively. "Don't have time for that today."

"Do not mock me, Tennyson," orders the HighBreed Earth Commander as his DNAlien minions slowly move into position around the intruders. "You can die quickly, with the rest of your insignificant race, or slowly, at my hands."

"Or," Swampfire offers, "I was thinking, not at all. Call it off."

"Foolish children," spits the HighBreed Commander. "Enough of this!" He turns to the DNAliens. "Destroy the other two. Leave Ben 10 to me."

Obediently, the DNAliens barrel forward to attack the trespassers. Stone Kevin knocks the first two out. Gwen uses her martial arts training to kick a couple more.

While Kevin and Gwen take on the DNAliens in hand-to-hand combat, Swampfire rushes at their boss. But as soon as Ben's creature gets within arm's length, the HighBreed Earth Commander lands a big punch, splattering Swampfire's head! He crumples to the ground.

"No!" cries Gwen.

CHAPTER EIGHT

The HighBreed Earth Commander stands over Swampfire, proclaiming triumphantly, "And so, it ends. Just as your grandfather destroyed himself trying to defeat me, so you too fall at my . . . "

While the HighBreed goes on and on, the vines at Swampfire's neck rustle to life and begin to intertwine, threading together to reform Swampfire's head! The first words out of his regenerated mouth are, "I'm kind of mad now."

Swampfire sits up and blasts the startled HighBreed with a two-handed stream of fire.

Another HighBreed joins the fight, leaping at Gwen, who quickly protects herself with an energy dome. As this HighBreed prepares to smash Gwen's shield, Stone Kevin taps him on the shoulder. "Hey."

When the HighBreed turns to look, Stone Kevin hits him with a big, two-handed blow that knocks him clear across the room. He lands on a control panel, destroying it in an explosion that blasts him back into the middle of the floor. Kevin runs over to throw another punch, but the HighBreed's hand shoots up and catches Kevin's hand, then grabs Kevin around the chest and begins to squeeze. Kevin's protective stone shell starts to crumble!

Swampfire has his hands full trading big punches with the HighBreed Earth Commander. Slowly but surely, Swampfire is being driven backward. Swampfire is putting up a good fight, but this HighBreed is stronger than he is!

The other HighBreed is smashing Kevin through tables and consoles, again and again. Kevin's stone armor is being chipped away by every impact! First Kevin's arm, then his shoulder, then his whole head is exposed. The HighBreed reaches out and grabs Kevin in one hand. Kevin struggles to get away.

"Leave him alone!" Gwen's voice calls out.

The HighBreed holding Kevin looks over to Gwen.

"Very well. I was nearly done with him anyway." He tosses Kevin aside like a rag doll and stalks toward Gwen.

Gwen puts up a thick energy shield bubble to protect herself, but the HighBreed shatters it with one punch! "That won't keep me from you, vermin."

Gwen staggers back, obviously weakened, as the HighBreed continues, "Or perhaps I'll finish your friend first." He indicates Kevin, lying unconscious on the floor. "So you can watch him suffer."

The HighBreed heads back toward helpless Kevin. Gwen tries to project energy to stop him, but it fizzles in her hands.

"Yes, you're no threat to me now," scoffs the HighBreed, lifting a Kevin by one ankle and dangling him above the ground. The HighBreed raises his hand to deliver the final blow.

"I said . . . " Gwen's voice growls. The HighBreed turns around to see manna rippling the air in front of Gwen. "Leave him alone!" As she speaks, Gwen's voice distorts and deepens. Her body is being consumed by an overwhelming wave of manna. Gwen has become pure energy!

Gwen gestures at the HighBreed threatening Kevin.

An energy beam arcs toward the villain, blowing him right through the wall and outside into the night sky!

Energy Gwen hovers in the air, shimmering. Kevin struggles to get up. "Gwen?" He limps over to her floating energy form and grabs onto her by the shoulders.

"So much power!" gushes Energy Gwen.

"Gwen, listen to me," pleads Kevin. "You've got to shut it down."

"No," she insists, "I think I can defeat the HighBreed all by myself!"

"Your grandmother said it would take at least seventy-five years for you to master that power," Kevin reminds her.

"We don't have seventy-five years," she responds.

"You'll lose your humanity," begs Kevin. "You won't remember Ben, or me." Kevin holds Energy Gwen firmly by the shoulders. "Ben'll find another way to win. You've got to come back to me, Gwen. I can't lose you, okay?"

Energy Gwen's glow begins to waver. The over-abundance of manna is slowly drawn back inside her. A moment later, she is herself again. She looks up at Kevin, who smiles.

"Okay." Gwen answers, collapsing into his arms.

The battle between Swampfire and the HighBreed Earth Commander is still raging. The creature's brutal blows knock Swampfire to the floor. "You're finished, insect!" declares the HighBreed, balling up his fist for the final strike.

"Not quite," says Swampfire. He opens his fist to reveal a handful of seeds, which he tosses onto the floor at the HighBreed's feet. The seeds grow at incredible speed into thick green vines, twining up and around the HighBreed Earth Commander's body. A moment later, he is trapped in place.

Swampfire grins. "Okay, *now* I'm finished. And as soon as you give the order, the whole invasion's over."

At this, the HighBreed laughs heartily.

"You think this is funny?" Kevin asks, joining Swampfire.

"I don't have the authority to call off the invasion," the HighBreed Commander explains. "Only the HighBreed Supreme could end the attack, and he is beyond your reach, safe on the home world."

"Well," Kevin says, "at least things can't get any worse."

As if on cue, dozens of armed DNAliens swarm the chamber.

"Ah, man!" Swampfire sighs.

"I'll try shoving them back with a shield," says Gwen. "Maybe we can—"

She is interrupted by loud fight noises coming from behind the DNAliens. Suddenly, one of the DNAliens is thrown forward to the ground, then another, and another!

"One side, alien freaks! You're in my way!" a voice shouts.

Gwen recognizes that voice. "Manny!"

Manny comes crashing through the crowd, man-handling the DNAliens, punching, shoving, and tossing them aside. He is a young, red, muscular creature similar to one of Ben's past alien forms, Four Arms. Manny is a member of a group called the Plumbers' Helpers. The last time Ben and Gwen saw him, he was working with Grandpa Max in the Null Void.

"Hey, Gwen," Manny replies, casually tossing aside another DNAlien.

Before Gwen can respond, a blur zigzags through the room, snatching the laser guns right out of the DNAliens' hands. The speedy creature zips to a stop near Manny. It's his partner, Helen. She's a thin, blue, superfast, creature similar to XLR8, another of Ben's past forms. She slides open her facemask and drops the armload of laser guns she just collected.

Now a third character flips into the room, rapid-firing needles from his hand like an automatic weapon. He aims at Helen's pile of laser pistols, destroying them in a fiery explosion. Then he lands with a flourish in the center of the room. It is Helen's brother, Pierce, yet another of the Plumbers' Helpers.

"Helen and Pierce?" Swampfire says, amazed. Then it dawns on him! "But that means . . ."

"How's it going, kids?" Grandpa Max enters the room through the hole Gwen made in the wall, riding on the back of a terrifying-looking flying Null Guardian. He pats the creature's head and dismounts. "Easy, boy."

Swampfire grins and rushes toward Max, transforming back into Ben on the run. He gets to his grandfather just in time to join Gwen and Max in a group hug.

"Grandpa Max!" Ben can't believe his eyes.

Manny makes four fists and poses, looking tough. "And Max Force!"

Grandpa Max frowns. "What did I say about calling us that?"

Manny just shrugs. "I think it sounds cool."

Gwen can barely contain her excitement. "What are you doing here? I thought you were going to stay in the Null Void until you cleaned it up."

"Pretty much got things under control there," her grandfather explains. "Anyway, after all the work I put into uncovering the HighBreed conspiracy, there is no way I am sitting out the final round."

"Then you've arrived just in time to see the end, Max Tennyson," intones the HighBreed Earth Commander from within the vines restraining him. "My fleet will uncloak and destroy the Earth in less than one of your hours."

"And we don't even have a plan," worries Kevin.

"Sure we do," says Ben. "The Hyperspace Jump Gate is like a door from the HighBreed home world to here, right?"

"Right," Kevin agrees. "So?"

"So a door out is also a door in," Ben finishes. He turns to Gwen. "Got your phone?"

Gwen looks puzzled. "Sure. Why?"

Outside on the battlefield, Cooper, Paradox, Azmuth, Darkstar, Heatblast II, and Julie are still zapping all the

DNAliens they can find. The combat is fierce, and HighBreed Destroyers fill the sky as far as the eye can see.

As laserfire rains down on her from all directions, Julie's cell phone rings. She ignores it. Who calls in the middle of a war?

Suddenly, Paradox appears next to her. "Aren't you going to answer it?" he asks Julie. "It's important."

Bewildered, Julie opens her cell. "Hello?" She listens intently for a moment then says, "Okay," and snaps her phone closed.

Paradox smiles. "Told you." Then he vanishes in a flash.

Back inside the Control Tower, Gwen is also closing her cell phone. She looks at Ben and nods. "All set."

"Great." Then he turns to Max and asks, "Grandpa? Can you hold the line here?"

Max replies, "Keep them from retaking the control room? Consider it done."

Ben heads for the hole in the wall that Gwen made earlier. Manny calls after him, "Where are you going?"

"Just stepping out for a second," Ben responds cryptically. With that, he steps out of the hole and drops straight down out of sight!

"Ben!" cries Grandpa Max.

A few seconds later, Ben rises slowly back up into view. He's standing on top of warship Ship!

"Shiiiiiip!" says Ship.

"Gwen. Kevin. You coming?" Ben calls.

Gwen and Kevin hurry over to the hole in the wall and hop out onto Ship.

Ben turns back to the friends they're leaving behind. "If we don't make it, it's up to you guys."

"Forget that, man," says Manny. "We'll see you when you get back." He gives Ben a triple thumbs-up.

Grandpa Max winks at Ben, who smiles back, then turns and follows Gwen and Kevin inside Ship.

On the battlefield below, Julie looks up from zapping more DNAliens to see Ship zooming through the night sky. "There they go!" she cheers. Then her expression changes. "Be careful, Ben," she whispers.

CHAPTER NINE

In the cockpit of warship Ship, Ben is at the controls. Kevin and Gwen are in the back row of seats. Azmuth is riding shotgun. The human-sized seatbelt pulled across him almost covers his whole body.

Ben grins as he steers the warship. "About time I got to drive."

Kevin gestures to Azmuth. "I'm still trying to figure out what Bug-eyes is doing here."

"If you're referring to me," Azmuth answers huffily, "surely you didn't believe I would leave the Omnitrix unprotected."

Gwen lays a hand on Azmuth's little shoulder. "Ben worries about you too."

Azmuth glares back at Gwen. "I am only concerned with the Omnitrix, not Ben."

"Of course you are," says Gwen condescendingly.

"Jump Gate coming up," Ben announces. "I'm going to change into my flight suit."

He dials the Omnitrix to Brain Storm's hologram, then slams his palm down. There's a flash of green, and Ben is gone. Sitting in the driver's seat is a big-headed, red, alien, shellfish-like Cerebrocrustacean who calls out his name: "Brain Storm!"

There's a pause, then Brain Storm announces, "With my oversized cranium and the intellectual superiority that naturally follows from it, this is obviously the correct form to pilot this vehicle under these trying conditions."

"That's precisely why I should pilot this ship!" Azmuth complains.

Brain Storm snorts derisively. He holds the tips of one of his claws about an inch apart in front of Azmuth's face, like a human holding his index finger and thumb apart to indicate something is teeny-tiny.

Azmuth is not amused. "Are you inferring that you're smarter than me because your head is bigger?"

"No." Brain Storm replies in his most patronizing

tone. "I'm implying that I'm smarter than you because my *brain* is bigger."

"Here's your chance to prove it," Kevin interrupts. "Incoming!" He points at the screen ahead.

In the sky in front of the Jump Gate, several HighBreed Destroyers break formation to intercept Ship. They are much bigger than he is, even in his current form.

Ship dodges laser fire from the HighBreed Destroyers while zigzagging past them. Then he barrel rolls between them, firing shots in every direction, tricking two HighBreed Destroyers into shooting each other down!

In the cockpit, Gwen asks Azmuth about the Jump Gate. "How does it work?"

"It converts you into faster-than-light tachyons," the Galvan starts to explain.

"Broadcasts them to the receiver Gate on the opposite side of the galaxy," interjects Brain Storm.

"Then reconstitutes you," finishes Azmuth.

Azmuth and Brain Storm look at each other and frown. Before anyone can say anything else, Ship flies under the arch and enters the Jump Gate.

Suddenly, they are no longer anywhere! A low, pulsing humming sound slowly builds to a crescendo. The

AGE: Fifteen

HOME WORLD: Earth

SPECIES: Human

ABILITIES: Ben can trade his own DNA for the DNA of ten different alien species using the Omnitrix, the most advanced piece of technology ever created.

LIKES: Smoothies, soccer, and hanging out with his girlfriend, Julie

Gwen Tennyson

AGE: Fifteen

HOME WORLD: Earth

SPECIES: Human

ABILITIES: Gwen holds a black belt in karate. She can manipulate energy fields to create shields or blast enemies. In addition, she can track people or objects by detecting their manna, the hidden energy that permeates all of nature.

LIKES: Doing research; shopping with Julie; Kevin

AGE: Sixteen

HOME WORLD: Earth

SPECIES: Human

ABILITIES: Ben's former nemesis can take on the substance of anything he touches — metal, wood, rubber, stone, etc.

LIKES: His car, a souped-up GTO; trading illegal alien tech; Gwen

Kevin E. Levin

HOME WORLD: Terradino

SPECIES: Vaxasaurian

ABILITIES: Humungousaur is physically the strongest of Ben's alien forms. He's also a size changer — he can grow to sixty feet tall.

HOME WORLD: Methanos

SPECIES: Methanosian

ABILITIES: Swampfire can shoot fire from his hands like a flamethrower. He's nearly impervious to physical harm: Projectiles pass harmlessly through him, and severed limbs can be reattached. Swampfire can also control the growth of nearby plant life and can regrow his entire body when needed.

HOME WORLD: Aeropela

SPECIES: Aerophibian

ABILITIES: Jet Ray can swim through the water or fly through the air at several times the speed of sound. Using his stinger, he's able to deliver powerful neuroshocks that can shut down an attacker's central nervous system.

HOME WORLD: No home planet; he was created by unpredictable cosmic storms

SPECIES: To'kustar

ABILITIES: Way Big is one of Ben's original alien forms, and he's definitely the biggest of the bunch. Reaching over one hundred feet tall, he's got enough power to take out an entire army.

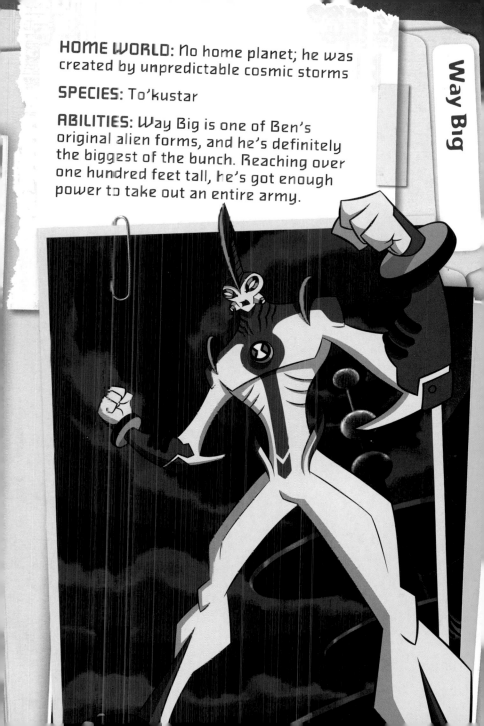

HOME WORLD: Arburia

SPECIES: Arburian Pelarota

ABILITIES: Cannonbolt looks clumsy at first, but when he curls up inside the thick armor on his back, he becomes an unstoppable wrecking ball. When he launches himself at high speeds, he can cause massive damage.

stars outside and all the humans and creatures inside elongate and blur. There is a bizarre color shift.

Gwen waves her hand in front of her face, enjoying the waves of multiple images. "Oooh! That's cool!" she says, her voice echoing strangely.

As Ship emerges from the other side of the Jump Gate, everything returns to normal again.

Azmuth exhales, "We've arrived."

"Is everybody okay?" asks Gwen as Kevin rubs his eyes.

Brain Storm is looking a little woozy. "I don't feel so good." He leans to the side and throws up!

Unfortunately, someone very little happens to be sitting under where Brain Storm just leaned. Azmuth is now covered with vomit!

The usually very proper Brain Storm is mortified. "Oh, my dear fellow! Sincerest apologies."

Suddenly, the cabin shakes, rattling everyone. Ship's deep voice calls out to his friends, "Ship!"

Kevin can guess what he's saying. "We've been hit!"

"Try and get us to the High Council Building, the tall one over there!" Azmuth yells over all the commotion.

Ship has sustained heavy damage. Trailing smoke, he careens through the gray skies over the HighBreed planet. He heads for the tallest building in sight but, zigzagging out of control, crashes through the side about halfway up.

Ship somehow manages to skid to a stop inside the building. Thick smoke billows around him. The gang-plank lowers. There is a green flash, and Ben stumbles out and collapses!

CHAPTER TEN

Things slowly come into focus as Ben blinks, waking up. "What happened?" he groans.

"A bunch of HighBreed guards caught us after we crashed," Kevin answers.

Looking around, Ben sees Kevin, Gwen, and Azmuth are shackled to the wall. Then he realizes he is too! The three humans are held in place by bands at their wrists, the Galvan by one of the same bands across his whole body.

"The good news is that we made it to the HighBreed's headquarters," Gwen says. They are in an eerie, cave-like chamber with support beams that look like thick underground roots and creepy, honeycombed patterns swelling from the floor.

"What about Ship?" asks Ben.

"He's okay," says Gwen. "I told him to hide until we called him."

Ben tests his shackles, straining to get at his left wrist. "If I could just reach the Omnitrix."

Azmuth shakes his head, sighing. "Why do you need to reach it?"

Ben remembers the voice recognition feature Azmuth recently unlocked for him. "Oh. Right." He gives the Omnitrix a verbal command. "Omnitrix: Humungousaur."

In a blinding flash of green light, Ben is transformed into his hulking Vaxasaurian form. "Humungousaur!" he calls out, his shackles bursting as he grows.

Humungousaur tears apart the wall behind Kevin and Gwen, freeing them. Kevin crouches down and absorbs the alien metal from the floor, then uses his enhanced strength to snap off the one metal wrist shackle restraining Azmuth.

Out in the corridor, two HighBreed Guards approach to investigate the noise. But before they can enter, Humungousaur's gigantic fist punches the door down, knocking the two guards aside!

Humungousaur grabs one of the guards for questioning. Gwen approaches him, powering up magenta energy on both of her hands. Metallic Kevin, with Azmuth on his shoulder, steps in behind her.

"Hi," Gwen says cheerfully to the HighBreed in Humungousaur's grip. "Take us to your leader."

A few minutes later, the HighBreed guard bursts through a door and lands at the feet of the five other HighBreed. One of these HighBreed has different facial markings than the others, plus a strange glowing pattern on his chest. "Who dares!" bellows the HighBreed Supreme Commander.

In strides Humungousaur, Gwen, and Metallic Kevin with little Azmuth standing on his shoulder.

The HighBreed guard scrambles to his feet before his superior. "I'm sorry, master, they took me by surprise—"

The HighBreed Supreme Commander holds up a hand. The guard is instantly silent. He bows and walks away. The Supreme HighBreed peers at Humungousaur. "You are the Earth vermin, Ben 10?"

"Ben Tennyson. Yeah," answers Humungousaur. "You're the HighBreed top banana, right?"

"I've read reports of your tenacity," muses the supreme leader, "but truly, your gall exceeds all description."

Humungousaur takes that as a compliment. "Thanks." Then he pushes his luck. "I want you to call off the attack on Earth."

The HighBreed Supreme Commander is amused. "Just like that?"

"Pretty much," says Humungousaur. "What have you got to gain by hurting us?"

"You are mongrels," states the head HighBreed, "inferior life-forms. Your very existence is an affront to our purity."

Azmuth speaks up from Kevin's shoulder. "Can we dispense with these lies?"

The Supreme Commander recoils. "You accuse me of dishonesty? Your race is the Galvan, correct? A slightly more intelligent form of pond scum."

"Don't be fooled by his posturing, Ben," counters Azmuth. "They aren't attacking because of their supposed 'superiority.' They're attacking because they're dying out. Their ridiculous belief in 'racial purity' led to inbreeding, a loss of resistance to disease, and finally sterility." Azmuth looks up at the gigantic HighBreed, not at all intimidated. "This is the last generation of HighBreed, is it not?"

"You are correct, vermin," replies the head HighBreed. "But we will not perish alone."

A screen overhead winks to life, displaying images of different planets as well as the HighBreed armada in space.

The leader continues, "In a matter of hours my fleet will destroy not just Earth, but every known inhabited planet in this galaxy!"

The green planet of Galvan appears onscreen. Our heroes watch as cracks spread across its surface. Then the whole planet glows a terrible red from within. The whole planet looks like it's about to explode into dust!

"The fall of Galvan was the signal for our final attack to begin," the Supreme Commander declares. "Enjoy the view. You are about to witness the end of all life in the universe!"

CHAPTER ELEVEN

Azmuth slumps in defeat. "All is lost. They are far too powerful to fight."

But Humungousaur has an idea. "Why fight them when we can help them?" Humungousaur speaks to the symbol on his chest. "Omnitrix, can you repair the genetic damage to the HighBreed? All of them?"

The green hourglass shape blinks and speaks in Ben's voice. "Genetic manipulation on that scale will require all available power."

In a flash of green energy, Humungousaur is gone. Ben stands in his place, looking at the Omnitrix pulsing green on his wrist. It speaks to him in his own voice again. "Genetic recombination sequences ready."

The Supreme HighBreed is suspicious. "What are you doing?"

Ben holds his left fist in the air. "Wait for it. . . ."

On his wrist, the face of the Omnitrix glows a more powerful green than ever before. Inside, its swirling stew of DNA bubbles and crackles, roiling until its energy explodes out of the watch in an ever-expanding circular wave. It passes harmlessly through Ben and his friends, but turns the HighBreed green as it passes over them. The pulse travels right through the walls and out into the HighBreed home world!

The circular wave of green energy emanates from the top of the Highbred Command Center building, washing out over the landscape and illuminating every HighBreed it touches. When the pulse of energy reaches the Jump Gate on the HighBreed home world, it activates!

In Los Soledad, Paradox, Cooper, Julie, and Heatblast pause in their Bugzapping duty as a wave of intense energy comes pouring through the Jump Gate! It passes harmlessly through all of them. Even the DNAliens are unaffected by it.

But up in the HighBreed control tower, the HighBreed Commander, still trapped in place by Swampfire's vines, flashes green as it strikes him!

Back on the HighBreed planet, all is still. The energy wave is gone.

Inside the HighBreed Command Center, the Supreme leader is livid. "What have you done?" His appearance has changed—he is now red with yellow spots. The other HighBreed in the room are also now all different colors instead of their usual white with purple markings.

Ben explains, "I ordered the Omnitrix to reprogram your DNA."

Kevin nods approvingly. "And judging from the new look, I'd say it worked."

Ben double checks. "Omnitrix?"

The Omnitrix answers him in his own voice, "Program complete. All HighBreed in range of transmission are now genetically fused with random species from Omnitrix database."

"In range of transmission!" the HighBreed Supreme Commander says incredulously. "With the Jump Gates open for the attack—"

Azmuth smiles smugly, "Every HighBreed in the galaxy is now a . . . how did you put it?"

"He called us mongrels," Gwen supplies helpfully.

"Welcome to the kennel club," Kevin says smugly.

The Supreme leader is crushed. "How could you do this?"

Ben is confused. "I don't understand. I saved you."

"You have made us impure," the Supreme HighBreed groans. "There is only one honorable act left to us."

"No!" shouts a familiar voice. "There is another way!"

Reinrassig III bursts into the chamber. He is a HighBreed with one irregular green arm, given to him by Swampfire during a survival adventure on a desert planet.

"Reiny!" Ben blurts out.

Gwen is surprised. "You know him?"

Ben shrugs. "I know a lot of people."

Reinrassig raises his green arm and addresses his Supreme leader and the rest of the council. "This human once cured an ailment of mine by changing my DNA. At first I thought the impurity a curse, but I have since learned otherwise. Fellow HighBreed, we can live!"

For a moment or two, the altered HighBreed speak to each other conspiratorially in an alien tongue Ben, Gwen, and Kevin cannot understand. Then the red HighBreed Supreme Commander turns to Reinrassig and announces, "It is decided. The High Council elects *you* HighBreed Supreme. Lead us wisely."

Reiny bows low. "I will try."

Outside the tower, the voice of Reinrassig, the new Supreme leader of all the HighBreed, fills the air. Thanks to a transmitter, it is even heard by the HighBreed armada in space. "To all HighBreed within the sound of my voice. The war is over. Return home so we can create a new future together."

Reinrassig turns and offers his open hand to his former enemy. "Thank you for your help, Benbentennyson."

Ben can't help but smile at the name Reiny always calls him. The HighBreed and the human shake hands.

CHAPTER TWELVE

Back in Los Soledad, the final HighBreed Destroyer flies through the arch into the Jump Gate.

Ben watches them go. "That's the last of them."

The portal powers down. Grandpa Max puts his arm around Ben and smiles up at the departing fleet.

"It's a beautiful sight, isn't it?" says Max. Then he takes a hand grenade out of his satchel, pulls the pin, and tosses it at the top of the arch. The grenade explodes, splitting the arch in half and causing a chain reaction of smaller explosions that travel down both arms of the arch, destroying the structure bit by bit until there is nothing left. A final explosion removes any trace of it.

Grandpa Max sees Kevin's curious look and tells him, "Fusion grenade."

Kevin is impressed. "Nice."

Julie looks at her watch. "I've got to go home. Since it's not the end of the world, I'm still under curfew."

Ben takes Julie's hands tenderly in his. Feeling self-conscious, he looks over and sees Kevin, Gwen, and Grandpa Max staring at him, smiling.

Ben 10, wielder of the Omnitrix, savior of the universe, bravely says to his girlfriend, "Okay, walk you to school tomorrow."

Julie heads up the gangplank into warship Ship, pausing for one last little wave to Ben before she goes.

Then Ship rises into sky, rotates, and zooms away.

Gwen turns to Max and asks hesitantly, "Grandpa, are you going back to the Null Void?"

"No," Max replies, glancing over at Manny, Helen, Pierce, Cooper, and Alan. "After watching Ben's recruits in action, I think they need some training from an old pro." Grandpa Max smiles at Ben, Gwen, and Kevin. "You three sure don't need me any more."

Ben hugs him. "I'll always need you, Grandpa."

Max shouts over to the Plumbers' kids, "C'mon, team, you're with me."

Manny picks up Cooper and they hurry over to their new leader.

Max smiles as he assesses the bunch of recruits. "Ooh, I'm gonna need a bigger motor home." Then he climbs onto the back of the Null Guardian and flies off.

Ben realizes someone's unaccounted for. "What happened to Darkstar?"

"He snuck away during all the excitement," reports Gwen. "We'll get him."

"But not today." Kevin looks wistfully at the smoldering remains of his beloved car. "Today I'm going to the auto show. I need a new ride."

Gwen steps up beside him. "I'll go with you."

"You like cars?" Kevin asks her, surprised.

"Not really," she admits. "I like you, though."

Kevin smiles and offers her his elbow. They walk away together.

Ben, Paradox, and Azmuth are the only ones left.

"Nice working with you again, Ben," says the Professor sincerely. "It's time to take Azmuth home."

Azmuth agrees. "There's a lot of rebuilding to do back on Galvan."

Ben has one more thing he needs to ask the creator of the Omnitrix. "Before you go, can you reengage the master control? That DNA wave I made seems to have reset it."

Ben rolls up his sleeve and holds out his Omnitrix wrist to Azmuth, who just smiles. "Yes. It has, hasn't it? Have fun figuring it out."

With that, Azmuth and Paradox disappear in a flash.

Ben is left alone, looking at the Omnitrix. He scrolls through several images very quickly. "Aw, man. I don't recognize any of these guys!" Then his frown turns to an adventurous grin.

Ben 10 selects a brand-new creature and slams the Omnitrix, and there's a brilliant flash of green light. "Oh well, here we go again!"

Want to read more about
Ben 10 Alien Force?
Check out this exclusive
excerpt from the
Ben 10 Alien Force
movie novelization,
in stores October 2009.

CHAPTER ONE

Vrooooooooooooooom . . .

The sound of a souped-up engine bounced off of the snowy hillsides surrounding the picturesque town of Bellwood. A bright green muscle car raced out of town, headed for a deserted mill in the middle of nowhere.

The car screeched to a stop outside the mill and the teenage driver got out. Kevin Levin's shaggy dark hair hung over his brown eyes. He looked tough in jeans, a black T-shirt, and a black short jacket. As he strode into the open space of the empty mill, a man with greasy hair approached him.

"What've you got for me, Fitz?" Kevin asked.

"I knew you'd be the guy to call on this, Kev, because it's big and I need to move it," Fitz said. He sounded nervous. "I figured you'd have the connections to—"

"Show me," Kevin said impatiently.

Fitz took out a cell phone and sent a text message. Seconds later, three Japanese motorcycles raced into the mill, surrounding Kevin and Fitz. They screeched to a stop. All three riders wore black leather pants and jackets with matching black helmets.

Two of the riders took off their helmets and approached Kevin. They were both young guys, and each was holding a sleek metal briefcase. The third rider hung back in the shadows.

"You the buyer?" one of the guys asked.

"Depends," Kevin replied. "What are you selling?"

"Alien technology," the guy said. "The good stuff."

He opened the lid of his briefcase and pulled out a clear glass tube secured with aluminum caps on each end. Inside the tube were what looked like a bunch of tiny microchips.

Kevin wasn't impressed. "Uh-huh. So? What are they?"

The tech dealer looked surprised. "You don't know?"

Kevin rolled his eyes. "*You* don't know, do you?" he said. "Is it a weapon? Does it fire? Can it blow stuff up? This is important information to a prospective buyer."

"It's alien technology, man," the guy said. "It's got to be worth some cash. You interested or not?"

"Chill," Kevin said. He reached out to examine the glass tube. "Let me talk to my partners."

Fitz looked more nervous than ever. "Partners? You didn't say anything about partners."

"Neither did you," Kevin said coolly.

Gwen Tennyson, a sixteen-year-old girl with long, red hair, stepped into the mill. Another figure walked behind her, a slim teenage boy wearing jeans and a black T-shirt. A green device that looked like a high-tech watch was strapped to his wrist.

Fitz went pale. "Uh, you're working with him?"

Ben Tennyson stepped forward. "Actually, I'm working with her," he said, nodding to Gwen. "Kevin doesn't really work. He just stands around flexing his muscles."

"How about I flex them on your face?" Kevin joked.

The second biker stepped up to Gwen and looked her over. Then he turned to Fitz. "Who are these jokers, man?"

"I can't tell you," Fitz said. "I'm just the middleman."

Gwen focused her intense green eyes on the biker. She wasn't the least bit intimidated. "We're just some regular old folks who are beginning to think this is a big fat waste of our time," she said.

Ben nodded at the chips in the tube. "What've we got?" he asked Kevin.

"Never seen anything like 'em," Kevin replied. "They're complex. Possibly self-replicating. Must be . . . grade nine tech at least."

The two biker guys looked impressed. Kevin knew what he was talking about.

Suddenly, the green device on Ben's wrist started flashing and making beeping noises. Ben messed around with some of the dials on it, but couldn't stop it.

"Whatever they are, they're screwing with the Omnitrix," Ben said, shaking his head.

"What's up with you guys? Never met dealers like you before," said the first biker.

The third biker finally spoke. Her voice was feminine but tough.

"You never met *anyone* like them before," she corrected him, "because they're not just black-market lowlifes like you. They're Plumbers."

The biker was confused. "You mean they're going to pay for this stuff by fixing my toilet?"

The girl biker took off her helmet. Dark hair spilled across her face.

"The Plumbers are a secret interplanetary security force. Saving the world so we don't have to." From the tone of her voice, it was clear she didn't like Plumbers very much.

Kevin tried to play it off. One of the important things about being a Plumber was keeping your secret job just that — a secret.

"Yeah, right. Of course. We're cops from outer space," he said. "Or maybe we're firemen from Atlantis."

Ben was curious. There was something familiar about the girl's voice. "How did you learn about these 'Plumbers' you think we are?"

"Everything I know about the Plumbers I learned the same way you did . . . Ben," the girl shot back.

Ben and his cousin Gwen exchanged glances. How did she know about the Plumbers? And how did she know Ben's name?

The girl finally stepped into the light. Her pretty face was marred by an angry scowl.

Ben's eyes went wide. "Elena?"

"No way," Gwen said.

"Who?" Kevin asked.

"Oh, you still remember me. I'm honored," Elena said sarcastically.

Kevin looked at Ben and Gwen. "Hello? Anybody want to toss me a clue about what's going on here?"

"Kevin, this is Elena Validus," Gwen said. Her voice was as frosty as the winter air. "She's a Plumber's kid, like us."

"Not like you, Gwen," Elena pointed out. "None of my ancestors were aliens. I don't have any cool powers to rely on."

"We hung out for a while back in the day," Ben told Kevin. "Then Elena's dad quit." He nodded to Elena. "Then you moved away and we haven't heard from you since."

Elena's eyes flashed with anger. "Is that what they told you? That my dad quit? Considering you've got more power than all of the Plumbers combined, you don't know much."

"Then why don't you tell me. What's going on?" Ben asked. "What are you doing here with these chips?"

"I'm here to find you," Elena said, and her voice softened a little. "The Plumbers don't exactly advertise. I need your help, Ben. It's my father. He's been abducted."

"Call the cops," Kevin suggested.

"They can't help," Elena snapped. "His disappearance is connected with these alien chips."

"We'll help you find him, Elena," Ben said earnestly. "You're a Plumber's kid and a friend."

"Am I, Ben? Really? Because life's been pretty hard for us the last three years, and I don't recall you ever looking us up," Elena said.

Before Ben could reply, a strange buzzing noise interrupted them.

"What is that?" Gwen asked. She looked at Elena accusingly. "Elena?"

"I don't know," Elena told her.

Inside the glass tube, the alien chips suddenly came to life. They buzzed and vibrated like a swarm of living insects. Together they threw themselves at the glass, trying to get out.

"It's a double cross," Kevin said.

Gwen grabbed her cousin's arm. "It's a trap, Ben."

"No, I swear it," Elena said. "I just wanted your help."

Fitz was sweating. "Well, I don't want to impose on your little dysfunction, so . . ."

Bam! The tube exploded. Chips flew in all directions. The two tech dealers dropped their briefcases and jumped back.

Bam! Bam! Bam! The other tubes exploded. Chips from each tube seemed to be drawn together. Soon there was one large swarm of chips buzzing above their heads like an alien rain cloud.

"Kevin, I think you were probably right about these not being ordinary computer chips," Ben quipped.

Above them, hidden in the rafters of the mill, a figure in a dark trenchcoat and hat watched the scene below. He raised his hands in the air in front of him like a symphony conductor. The swarm of alien chips moved when he moved. He was controlling them.

"Bring them back to ussssssss," the stranger hissed.

The mass of chips zoomed down like a swarm of bees.

They were under attack!

CHAPTER TWO

Thinking fast, Ben grabbed an old steel girder hanging from the ceiling. Wielding it like a baseball bat, he swung at the approaching swarm.

Whack! The blow sent many of the chips scattering—but now another swarm was headed for his cousin.

"Gwen!" he yelled.

Gwen did a quick backflip, springing out of the way. But the chips countered by forming a huge blob that was big enough to flatten her.

Gwen held out her hands, and a bubble of powerful pink energy shot out from them. The massive blob of chips crashed into Gwen's energy shield and shattered.

"Ben, I don't mean to backseat drive, but this might be a good time for the Omnitrix," Gwen called, her voice tense.

Ben looked down at the Omnitrix. Its lights were flashing out of control.

"Or not," Ben replied. "I think it's having a meltdown or something."

Another blob of chips had formed, ready to strike.

"Don't sweat it, dude," Kevin said. "If you can't handle it . . ." He touched one of the steel beams. Instantly, his whole body turned to steel. He kicked the blob, scattering the chips around the mill. The chips he'd destroyed fell to the floor like rain.

". . . I know someone who can!" Kevin bragged.

Ben snatched some of the dead chips from the ground. "They're not just chips," he reported. "It's some kind of alien nanotechnology."

"The attack is too organized," Gwen agreed. As she spoke, she sliced through clouds of chips with pink energy blades. "There must be some kind of intelligence behind it."

The last of the chips grouped together and flew at Elena and the two bikers. As she ducked out of the way,

Elena glanced up at the rafters. A look of shock crossed her face.

Ben followed her eyes. He spotted the shadowy figure moving his arms to control the chips.

"I don't know if he's intelligent, but I think we've found the puppeteer," Ben remarked.

The chips formed two large, razorlike blades. They zipped toward Ben, Gwen, and Kevin. As they flew, they sliced right through two steel columns. The columns toppled over, nearly taking out Elena and Fitz.

The two tech dealers jumped on their bikes and sped toward the mill entrance. A wall of chips blocked their way. The bikers quickly turned and crashed through a glass wall. They raced off into the distance.

"Too bad they had to leave before the main event," Ben said. He spun the dial on his Omnitrix. The device on Ben's wrist contained the DNA codes for aliens from all across the universe. With the Omnitrix, Ben could change into any of the forms he chose at will. And he knew just the right alien for this job. "Come on, Spidermonkey!"

A small hologram of Spidermonkey beamed from the Omnitrix. Ben slammed on the device's dial. Green light covered his body as he transformed . . . into Big Chill!

The Omnitrix had messed up—but why?

Big Chill had a blue humanoid body, a face like an insect, and large wings.

"This is so not Spidermonkey," Ben said in Big Chill's raspy voice.

"Less talking, more freezing," Kevin called out.

Big Chill flew at the last swarm of chips. They passed right through his ghostly form and instantly froze. The chips that survived tried to pull together for another attack, but they shattered against one another.

The chips rose overhead and formed a swirling tornado. Gwen fired a round of energy blasts at them. "A little help here?"

Big Chill flew toward the spiral of chips, blasting them with a powerful shot of freezing breath. This time, the frozen tornado shattered completely. Dead chips rained down on the mill floor.

"Thanks," Elena said.

"No problem," Big Chill replied.

The few chips that survived the blast flew up to

the rafters. The figure in the trenchcoat was still there, watching them.

"Who is that, Elena?" Kevin asked.

"Who's controlling all this?" Gwen wondered.

"I . . . don't know," Elena said hesitantly.

"Then let's find out," Big Chill said.

He zoomed up to the rafters and fired a freezing blast at the mysterious figure. The rafter exploded and the figure jumped off, hurling a ball of alien chips at Big Chill.

Big Chill ducked, and the ball landed on the ground right in front of Gwen.

Boom! Gwen went flying backward.

"Gwen!" Kevin ran to her and cradled her in his arms.

Big Chill morphed back into Ben. He approached his cousin.

"Gwen, you okay?"

Gwen sat up. "Yeah, I'm fine."

"Who is that guy?" Kevin asked.

The mysterious figure was nowhere to be seen. Above them, a small cloud of chips exited through the open skylight.

"I think you mean, who *was* he?" Ben replied. Then he turned, panicked. "Elena!"

But there was no sign of Elena either.

"If you're looking for your girlfriend, I think your personal charm was too much for her," Kevin said.

"Kevin's right," Gwen said. "She set us up."

"Did she?" Ben wondered. "I'm not so sure."